THE
HOLY SPIRIT

THE GREATEST PROMISE
AND THE GREATEST GIFT OF ALL

THE
HOLY SPIRIT

THE GREATEST PROMISE
AND THE GREATEST GIFT OF ALL

JOHN GITHIGA

ReadersMagnet, LLC

The Holy Spirit: The Greatest Promise And The Greatest Gift Of All
Copyright © 2021 by John Githiga

Published in the United States of America
ISBN Paperback: 978-1-953616-56-2
ISBN eBook: 978-1-953616-57-9

All rights reserved. No part of this publication may be reproduced, stored in a retrieval system or transmitted in any way by any means, electronic, mechanical, photocopy, recording or otherwise without the prior permission of the author except as provided by USA copyright law.

The opinions expressed by the author are not necessarily those of ReadersMagnet, LLC.

ReadersMagnet, LLC
10620 Treena Street, Suite 230 | San Diego, California, 92131 USA
1.619.354.2643 | www.readersmagnet.com

Book design copyright © 2021 by ReadersMagnet, LLC. All rights reserved.
Cover design by Ericka Obando
Interior design by Shemaryl Tampus

OTHER BOOKS BY THE AUTHOR

THE SPIRIT IN THE BLACK SOUL

CHRIST AND ROOTS:
Jesus As Revealed in the Bible and African Traditional Religions

INITIATION AND PASTORAL PSYCHOLOGY:
Toward African Personality Theory

THE SCRETETS OF SUCCESS IN MARRIAGE

25 SECRETS OF SUCCESS IN MARRIAGE

30 SECRETS OF SUCCESS IN MARRIAGE:
A Book for Premarital and Marriage Counseling

MINISTRY TO ALL NATIONS:
A Practical Theology of Mission and Church Planting

FROM VICTORY TO VICTORY

SYSTEMATIC THEOLOGY:
An Introduction To the African Theological Voice

THE FRUITFUL FAMILY:
Family Therapy Based on Christian Principal

ABOUT THE AUTHOR

Professor John Githiga is Patriarch of All Nations Christ Church International which is association of churches and ministry with the presence in every continent and founder, Chancellor and CEO of ANCCI University which is interdenominational and international. He is former Chaplain and faculty at West Texas A&M University where he taught Biblical studies and was President of United Campus Ministries. He is former chaplain and lecturer at Grambling State University where he taught Swahili and African philosophy and started KWANZA celebration. He was instructor at Pensacola Junior College where he taught in the department Humanity. He lectured on humanity in ancient world. Humanity and art and humanity and technological society. He was the head of the Department of Pastoral Theology at St. Paul's University(Kenya) where he taught pastoral theology and human background to pastoral ministry. He is founder and first president of the African Association for Pastoral Study and Counseling. He presided over Congress on Pastoral studies which was held at Democratic Republic of Congo. He is a graduate from Church Army College, St. Paul's United Theological College, Makerere University, the University of the South, Vanderbilt University and the International Bible Institute and Seminary. He holds a Diploma of Theology, Master of Divinity, Doctor of Ministry, Doctor of Religious Education, Doctor of Divinity. He is a student of theology, sociology, psychology, cultural anthropology and humanity. He was featured in the 2008-2009 edition of Madison Who's Who in Executives and Professionals having demonstrated exemplary achievement and made distinguished contributions to the business community. He is married to the Rev. Dr. Mary Githiga.

ABOUT THE BOOK

The book gives unprecedented insight for marriage enrichment and counseling by drawing wisdom from successful marriages in North America, Europe, Asia and Africa. The author interviewed hundreds of couples from these continents. The responder who included Christians, Muslims, Hindus Native American African American and Africans were couples who have been married for 10 to 70 years. They revealed the secrets of their success and the challenges which were facing as married partners. In addition, the author who have been married for 53 the same wife, reveals the secretes of their success. Thus, the book enables you to identify the causes of failure and to discover the secrets of success in marriage and is therefore of unsurpassed value to married partners and those who intend to marry and is a great tool for premarital counseling and marriage enrichment seminars.

DEDICATION

This book is dedicated to my brothers and sisters and companion in the suffering and kingdom and patient endurance that are ours in Jesus and to all those who faithfully serve God in the power of the Holy Spirit; to my two sisters, Jael Kibui Churu, Mary Wambui Mirara and my nephew, Isaac Githiga Methu.

ACKNOWLEDGEMENT

I am most grateful to my dear wife, the Rev.Dr. Mary Githiga for being the most faithful companion and helper, and Dr. Glen Sanborn, Chancellor of All Nation Christian Church International and Isaac Githiga, our Son, for proofreading this book.

CONTENTS

1. INTRODUCTION 1
2. THE GREATEST PROMISE 5
3. WE GIVE WHAT WE HAVE RECEIVED 9
4. YOU WILL RECEIVE POWER 17
5. SIGNS AND WONDERS 21
6. THE RADIANCE OF THE HOLY SPIRIT 23
7. SUFFERING AND GLORIFICATION 27
8. THE HOLY SPIRIT IN PADRE PENDA 33
9. PASTRORAL SEMINAR IN NAKURU HIGH 35
10. THE WORK OF THE HOLY SPIRIT 39
11. THE GIFTS OF THE HOLY SPIRIT 43
12. THE FRUIT OF THE HOLY SPIRIT 45
13. THE HOLY SPIRIT IN TRADITIONAL RELIGIONS 61
14. CONCLUSION 65

CHAPTER ONE

INTRODUCTION

THIS BOOK IS ABOUT how the Holy Spirit works in and through Church and will employ the African method of story-telling to communicate the eternal truth to the reader. It therefore entertains, soothes, challenges, and educates.

At the onset, we have to assert that the Holy Spirit is more than a subject. He is a person. He is seeing me and talking with me as I write about Him. He is also seeing you as you read this book. If you have not yet received Him, know that he is close to you that your nose is closer to your mouth. He desires to enter in you. He says: "Here I am! I stand at the door and knock. If anyone hears my voice and opens the door I will come in and eat with him, he with me." Revelation 3:20. When he comes in, not only are you forgiven of all your sin, but you are cleansed from all unrighteousness. You are justified. You are counted as though you have never sinned. Better still, He becomes your counselor, helper, comforter, and a dynamic power for witnessing and living a righteous life.

The Bible tells us that when you receive the Holy Spirit you will not be condemned, but you have passed from death to life. John 5:24. You are free from the law of sin and death, you only desire what the Spirit desires, your mind is controlled by the Spirit; the third person of the trinity replaces fear with courage:

> For you did not receive the spirit that make you a slave again to fear, but you received the Spirit of sonship. And by this we cry 'Abba, Father. The Spirit himself testify with our spirits that we are God's children. Now if we are children, then we are heirs- heir of God and co-heirs with Christ, if we indeed share in his suffering in order that we may share in His glory. Romans: 8: 1-17.

The author boldly confesses that the greatest gift that he received was the gift of the Holy Spirit when he was fifteen years old. So, my beloved, the greatest gift which you can receive is the Holy Spirit. Start with this; prayer:

> Spirit of the living God
> Fall afresh on me.
> Fills me. Mold me, melt me
> Spirit of the living God fall afresh on me.

I also encourage you to use the Collect of Day of Pentecost to pray for yourself and the universal Church,

> *Almighty God, on the day of Pentecost you opened the away of eternal life to every race and nation by the promised gift of the Holy Spirit: shed abroad this gift throughout the world by the preaching of the Gospel, that it may reach to the end of the earth; through Jesus Christ our Lord, who lives and reigned with you, in the unity of the Holy spirit, one God for ever and ever. Amen*

To fuel the fire of the Holy Spirit, start your day with prayer, reading of the Holy Scripture. My wife and I start the day by reading the scriptures using *Day by Day* published by *Forward Movement*. *It follows Daily Office* (you can google to get daily reading). This helps us to read four books of the Bible concurrently (two from the Old Testament and two from the New Testament). We complete the Bible within two years. *Daily Office* also enables us to cover the major doctrinal themes. We make a morning resolve which is as follows:

> *I will try this day to leave a simple, sincere, and serene life, repelling promptly every thought of discontent, anxiety, discouragement, impurity, self-seeking, cultivating cheerfulness, magnanimity, charity, and the habit of holy silence; exercising economy in expenditure, generosity in giving, carefulness in conversation, diligent in appointed service, fidelity to every trust, and childlike faith in God.*
>
> *In particular, I will try to be faithful in those habits of prayer, work, study, physical exercise, eating and sleep which I believe the Holy Spirit has shown me to be right.*
>
> *And I cannot by my own strength do this, nor with a hope of success attempt it, I look to thee O Lord God my Father, in Jesus my Savior, and ask for the gift of the Holy Spirit.*

When we talk, and write about the Holy Spirit, we need to ask the following questions: How can we speak of the Holy Spirit? Is he a subject for discussion or a living presence? Does he dwell in the trees, rocks, air, or in humankind? What is his work? What are his gifts? Does he give one gift to all believers? Does he bestow all his gifts upon every individual? Did the Holy Spirit exist in Africa long before the Missionaries came? Can we demarcate his revelation before and after the preaching of the gospel? If the Spirit is not alien to the African, why don't we allow him to express himself in African thought-form, language, expressions, and imageries?

This book addresses itself to the above questions and discusses the work, the gift, the fruits and the substance of the Holy Spirit. Since it is intended to be read by both theologian and laymen, it uses laymen's language. It uses the African method of teaching, that is, teaching through story-telling method. To even benefit more from this book, we ask you to pray using this prayer.

Almighty God
Our hearts are open before you,
Our desires are known to you,
And there is nothing we can hide from you,
Cleanse the thought of your heart
By the inspiration of your Holy Spirit,
That we may perfectly love you
And worthily magnify your Holy name. Amen

CHAPTER TWO

THE GREATEST PROMISE

THE HOLY SPIRIT IS the greatest promise in the bible. When our Lord Jesus was about to depart, He promised his disciples that he will not leave them as orphans: "I will ask the Father and He will give you another Counselor to be with you forever- the Spirit of the truth. John 14:16. Isaiah prophesied about the Spirit who will rest on the Messiah:

> The Spirit of the Lord will rest on Him-
> The spirit of wisdom and understanding,
> The spirit of counsel and power,
> The Spirit of knowledge and the fear of the Lord-
> He will delight in the fear of the Lord.
> He will not judge by what he sees or hear….
> But with righteousness he will judge the needy
> The wolf will lie with lamb,
> The lion will lie down with goat
> The infant will play near the hole of a cobra.
> They will neither harm or destroy on all my holy mountain.
> Isaiah 11:1-9.

God revealed to Isaiah the attributes of the Spirit who will rest in Messiah and the Messianic community. He is the Spirit of peace, love and unity. In the Messianic community, the strong will support the weak and the week will pray for the strong one- the wolf will lie down with a goat. The righteousness and peace will kiss each other. This community will seek to know the will of God by devoting themselves in fellowship and the study of the Holy Scriptures. This quality is found in the Apostolic Church. St Luke reports, "They devoted themselves in the apostolic teaching and to the fellowship, to breaking of bread and prayer." Acts 2:42. "Lions and goats" shared what they had, "selling their possessions and goods, they gave everyone as he had need." Acts 2:45.

Before he ascended our Lord, Jesus Christ promised the disciples, "But you will **receive powe**r when the **Holy Spirit** comes upon you and you will be my **witnesse**s in Jerusalem, and in all Judea and Samaria, and to the end of the earth." Acts 1:1. This indeed is the greatest promise in the Bible, since it was fulfilled a few days after was uttered by the Resurrected and Lord. These word words are as powerful as the last words of a parent. The words which he or she utter in the death bed. I still remember the last words of my father. After these words, I never saw him again. His words were: "All what I used to forbid, be free to do." He left us freedom. Nor curse. Those words have given me freedom of choice and freedom of movement and of interacting will all races and people of all categories. Different from my father, Jesus' promised coming of the Holy Spirit was fulfilled and within a few days.

On the day of Pentecost, the Holy Spirit fell mightily on the disciples, Luke reports,

> They were all together in one place. Suddenly a sound like a violent mighty wind came from heaven and filled the whole house where they were sitting. They saw what seemed to be tongues of fire that separated and come to rest on each of them. All of them were filled with the Holy Spirit and

began to speak in other tongues as the Spirit enabled them. Acts 2:6-8.

The Holy Spirit gave them the gift of tongue and the **gift of the ear**. Over the years Christians have emphasized tongue and forgotten ear. The Holy Spirit gives us both gifts. Astonished by the Spirit, the congregants asked, "Are not all these men who are speaking Galileans? How is it that each one of us hear them in our own native language?" Acts 2:6-8. This precious gift is the reverse of what happened at the tower of Babel. Genesis 11:1-9. The Holy Spirit brings people of many nations and races and tribes together and enables them to live together as brothers and sister. He facilitates communication.

The Holy Spirit gives us authority and power to witness and win people to Christ. Immediately after being filled with the Holy Spirit, Peter preached his first sermon and won three thousand to Christ. In his second sermon, he won five thousand to Christ. He was transformed from a fearful Peter, who denied his Lord three times, to Peter the Rock who, with enormous power, faced the supreme court who commanded him not to talk about Jesus. His bold response was, "judge yourself whether it is right to listen to you or listen to God." Acts 4: 18-19. Not only did he had power; he also had authority which gave him wisdom for using the dynamic power. He became a true witness of the Lord. The Greek word for witness means: *It doesn't matter what you will do with my body, as long as I have breath, I will not stop proclaiming Jesus as Lord.* Peter and other Apostles were ready to die for Christ. So many Christians have died for Christ. One of the recent cases was a story which was reported by Canon Andrew White who was ministering in Bagdad, Iraq. He tells of four children who ISIS members tried to force to deny Christ. The children responded to the most frightening creatures who had a butcher Knife: "Yoshua has always been good to us. And for that reason, we cannot deny Him." These children were beheaded. They didn't care what these killers had to do with their bodies. They did not do this on their own. They were empowered by the Holy Spirit.

It has to be borne in mind that transformation is a continuous process which starts with conversion - when we are convinced by the Holy Spirit of our sin, repent and then commit ourselves to Christ. Peter started with reaching out to Jews and eventually he went through a transformation when he was hungry on while on the roof praying. Acts 10: 9-10. Surprisingly, God was working on Peter as Trinity. His transformation started when he denied Christ three times. John 13: 38, Luke 22:34, Matthew 26:34. He was humbled. He wept. The second event was when Jesus asked him three times: Simon Son of John, do you truly love me more than this? Here Jesus was dealing with Peter's "better than thou attitude." Then Jesus told him, "feed my lamb." The third-time Peter was hurt because Jesus had asked him three times. John 21:16-17.

Peter thought that he was called to reach out to the Jews. A transformation took place when he was hungry on the roof of a house where he sees a vision with so many threes. He saw a large sheet with three categories of creatures: (1) four-footed animals; (2) reptiles; and (3) birds. He was told to do three things: (1) get up; (2) kill; and (3) eat. This happened three times. Acts 10:10-17. While he was wondering, what was happening, there three men appeared who were looking for him, sent by a Gentile soldier, Cornelius. Acts 10:18-22. Peter's sermon was directed to Peter: "You are all aware that it is against our law for a Jew to associate with a Gentile or visit him. But God has shown me that I should not call any man impure or unclean. Acts 10:27. Peter was a new man because he had done three things. "Get up. Kill. Eat. He had to take an action of killing his pride and was ready to move forward. Note that Cornelius had his "three." It was at three in the afternoon that an angel appeared to him and told him to call Peter. Acts 10:3. There is telepathic communication from both sides. This is really what happens to the community of the Risen Lord. When we are praying in Spirit God is also preparing a mission field for us. Said differently, when we're preparing to sow the seed, God is preparing the garden. And the seeds which we plant are what we have received.

CHAPTER THREE

WE GIVE WHAT WE HAVE RECEIVED

The Holy Spirit is the greatest promise our Lord Jesus promised the disciples that they will receive. John 14:14-16. In this chapter, we discuss this important promise using the person whom we name Padre Penda. The word Padre means 'father' Penda received this title from his mother for he is named after her father. Penda still remembers hearing this name when he was a toddler. If he was fussy and started crying, he waited to hear from mother, "Please be quite father." Padre Penda has received so much from many spiritual mothers and fathers and sisters and brothers. This is what he says,

> The more I reach out to all nations the more I realize that I only give what I have received. In retrospect, I realized that I have received much from many African communities. The East Africa Revival movement, which brought and nurtured me into the Christian faith, is comprised of all tribes in Kenya. My spiritual and professional parents include Hungarians, Dutchmen, Australians, the British, Canadians, and Americans. As the Bible, emphatically states, "To him who received more, more is required." The intension of the

mission journey to the United Kingdom and Kenya was to visit the people of God from whom I have received so much, including the Church in Kenya. I am most grateful to God who gave me the desire of my heart. The Holy Trinity also accorded me unspeakable traveling grace.

Ministry to all nations: Practical theology of Mission and Church Planting, p 212.

Penda committed himself to Christ when he was fifteen and started evangelizing when he was seventeen. He was giving gospel tracts and evangelizing on the street and market place in Nakuru and to hundreds of people when they were walking to work. Being so slim after being persecuted by deprivation of food, Penda believed that he was connected to universal Spiritual energy which was eminent and transcendent. He went wherever the Holy Spirit drove him feeling compelled to evangelize people of all categories, tribe and races. The following are a few of the dramatic episodes.

When he was seventeen, he was distributing gospel tracts. He was bare foot when he stopped a British (this was before Kenya was independent from the British nation and an African could only talk to a British when he was asking for a job). The teenager boy stopped the man and said, "Here is something for you which is small but most important." "No!" shouted the man. "Jesus loves the sinner but hate sin." The British shouted, "Do you understand the meaning of the word no?" "Yes I do, but I am telling you that Jesus loves you and is willing to save you." "I am going to put in prison!" the British man shouted louder! The Penda give him the last word, "First will be last and last first." They then parted and it is more than likely that the man committed himself to Christ. Penda's prophesy was fulfilled may years later when he consecrated a British bishop with a Spirit filled congregation comprising of seventeen nationality with evangelistic team which does street ministry as Penda was doing.

THE HOLY SPIRIT

Another humorous episode occurred when Penda was led by the Spirit to a Police village[1] with fifty-two homes. He was commanded by the Spirit to enter every home and tell the family whatever the Spirit will put in his mouth. As he entered a home, the fire of the Spirit was blowing in him. By the time he entered the fifth house he was intoxicated by the enormous Spirit energy. When he was getting out of the last home, a police officer asked him, "Who are you and who give you permission to enter police homes?' Penda announced, "I am son of the King of Kings and I was commanded by the King to do so." "Get away from here" shouted the officer! Penda departed with unspeakable joy.

It was not always safe for the Teenager-Penda to enter people's homes at night to preach the Gospel. On one occasion, the man who would not let him in said: "You are very lucky that you came when I have not taken my drugs. Otherwise you could not leave this place alive."

His housing was not always safe for a teenaged Penda who was living with his uncle who had placed penda with his coworker in a one-room apartment. On one occasion, the man, who cared nothing about the boy, told him that, "Tonight I am bringing a prostitute." He knew that Penda was very serious about his faith in Jesus, so that night the man brought home the prostitute. The only curtain between the man and his prostitute and Penda was darkness. When they started playing Jones, the boy started praying. The louder the bed cricked, the louder the boy prayed. Then the game turned into a fight. The man beat up his prostitute. In the morning, he left the woman with a teenager without giving her, her due. Penda then took his Bible and read the woman Revelation 19,

"After this I hear what sounded like the roar of the great multitude in the heaven shouting:

> Hallelujah!
> Salvation and power and glory belong to our God,

---

[1] A government supplied compound of homes for the families of police.

> For true and just are his judgments.
> He has condemned the great prostitute
> Who corrupt the earth by her adulteries.
> He has avenged on her the blood of servants.

Revelation 19:1-2. With lot of shame the woman left Penda and it more than likely that she committed herself to Christ like the Samaritan woman. John 4.

Penda was among many children who could not get access to high school. So, his uncle enrolled him in Nakuru Youth Club which offered technical courses. The boy took painting and signwriting. The boy noticed that no Religious Education was offered. So, he went to the Headmaster and asked him whether they could have RE. The Headmaster asked, "Are you going to teach?" "Yes sir!" Penda responded. Penda was told, "I will give 15 minutes to teach from Monday to Friday." The boy did it so well that that the Head Master gave him 50 minutes. So, all the teachers would leave at 11:10 and the students were left with Penda. He was so loved by the fellow students and was nicknamed "Bishop."

In the meantime, Penda was praying that God may open the door for him to get theological education. God answered his prayer! At the age of 21, The Right Reverend Neville Langford Smith, Bishop of Nakuru, enrolled him in Church Army, where he learned Evangelism and Urban Ministry. Upon completion of his training, the Bishop employed Penda to reach out to the street-children who were called, *watoto wa mapipa* - children of the dumpsite. Led by the Spirit, Penda has to venture into this challenging mission. For three months he was going onto the streets looking for these children without much success. On one occasion, he found a boy with dirt cloth and told the boy that he was looking for the boys who are unable to go to school. The boy responded, "You can get them in the dumpsite. If you go to the dumpsite and see that there are no birds. The boys are there."

THE HOLY SPIRIT

Going to the dumpsite, he found the boys. The following day he brought them popcorn. Eventually won them over and started meeting with them in his home which was located in Church compound. The sessions with them included each telling their own story. Most of the stories were about how they steal so as to survive. They would tell their stories until Penda listened with his mouth open. As he listened, a boy would take something from Penda's pocket and then ask, "Did you know when I took this? Then Penda would quickly check whether his wallet has been taken. Then the boy would announce, "We cannot take anything from you because you are our teacher." They and their parents all addressed Penda as "teacher." Surprisingly, for the five years that Penda ministered to these children, they never stole even a dime from him.

Eventually, Penda learned that there were several gangs who were calling themselves "battalions." There was the David Battalion, the Samson Battalion and the Cow-Brigadier Battalion. They adopted the names of movie characters. Penda befriended all the gang leaders and, through them, he got to most of the juvenile delinquents in the town.

Graciously, the Spirit used Bishop Neville to reach out to Oxfam International, which built the Center, and to the Municipal Council of Nakuru, which donated the building site. And thus, the boys were taken from the streets, from under the bridge, and from the prostitution homes, to a save Children Home. And Penda was Gazette[2] as government-approved-officer with a legal right of representing children in the law court. That meant that when children were arrested, Penda went and pleaded for their release with the promise that he will take care of the children in the Children Center.

---

[2] In Kenya, to be a "Gazette" meant having a legal right to protect and defend children at the court. In most, if not all, U.S. jurisdictions, a similar position is the *"guardian ad litem,"* a person appointed by a court to represent the "best interests of a child."

After getting thirty children, the Bishop added more staff. There were two teachers, a cook and a Church Army Captain. By this time Penda had married and the youngsters referred to his wife as "Madam."

There was more blessing when World Vision sponsored all the children. At this time Penda worked long hours doing the administration, keeping the books and guiding children to write thank you letters to the sponsor.

On one occasion Penda had a long day and walks home exhausted. As he looks at the neighborhood, he remembers how he used to have house to house visitation. He was asking himself - did I labor in vain? Reaching home, he found a lady with his wife who was taking a cup of tea. She appeared joyous and the tired Penda didn't know the source of her joy.

"Do you remember me?" asked the Lardy. "No." responded Penda. She inquired, "Don't you remember a group of women whom you preached to fifteen year ago?" "No. I don't remember." admitted Penda. The lady explained,

> "Let me tell you what you did. We were coming from school bare foot. You found five women and one of them was platting the hair of one of the women. You then stopped and said, "There is someone who is more precious than hair. Jesus Christ" I then cursed. And after cursing my hand was dislocated and couldn't finish working on the hair of my client. I went home with pain in my hand and told my daughter about a mad boy who preached to me. Then my daughter told me that I have committed a great sin because that boy is the man of God and that he is the one teaches them RE. When my daughter said that, I had thickness of heart and could not even swallow anything. And at the midnight, I committed myself to Christ. And from that time, I decided that I will be as crazy as that Boy. I became a street preacher and I have won so many people to Christ. One of the men whom I brought to Christ has brought more than

eight hundred persons to Christ. I have been looking for you for the last fifteen years and I am glad that I have found you."

Penda was so delighted and assured that some of the boys he ministers will become great men of God.

So, if you allow yourselves to be led by the Holy Spirit. You will bear fruits. To be in the Spirit is to be in Christ. Jesus put it this way: "I am the vine; you are the branches. If a man remains in me and I in him, he will bear much fruits, for apart from me you can do nothing." John 15:5. Not only that you will bear much fruit. But also, the fruit will remain forever. Let's hear more about the work of the Holy Spirit in Penda.

CHAPTER FOUR

YOU WILL RECEIVE POWER

The Risen Lord promised the disciples power. As we have seen, Penda, in the power of the Holy Spirit, was able to preach the gospel to all categories of people, police officers and their families, people on the streets and in their homes, Asians and Europeans, and juvenile delinquents. We also saw how Peter and the other apostles were transformed by the power of the Spirit of the Risen Lord. They were also given authority which gave them the wisdom of using this power according to God's will.

This power has two elements. It has the healing aspect which convinces people of their sins; which leads to confession and salvation. This power also has a destructive aspect which the theologian terms *herem,* which means "devoted for destruction so as to make it holy." It was this power that broke the chains and prison doors and led Peter out of prison. Acts 12: 6-10. It was also the same power impacting Ananias and Sapphira who lied to the apostle about the money. The two were struck dead. Acts 5: 1-10. Paul also used this power to confront Bar Jesus who was sabotaging Paul's mission to the Roman official. This man was blinded for a while. Acts 13: 7-12. This was the same *herem* that killed the first born of Egypt which made Pharaoh finally let the Israelites go. Exodus 12: 30-31. And it was the same power which broke the walls of Jericho. Joshua 6:1-27.

Interestingly, we were discussing the dynamic power in the Living Faith Church in Wigan, UK. Our bishop in Pakistan shared with us about what he understands about dynamic power. He believes that the power is of splitting the mountain. He shared with us how he used this power in Pakistan to stop Muslims from burning the church. In Pakistan, which has a Muslim-influenced government (the country's constitution refers to the Islamic Republic of Pakistan), Christians are not protected from sectarian extremists by the government and so our Bishop could only use the dynamic power of the Holy Spirit to stop burning of the church.

He called his pastors and evangelists and trained them how to use guns. When they were ready, the Bishop made a proclamation to the sectarian extremists: "For every church you burn, we will burn ten Mosques and for every Christian that you will kill, we will kill ten Muslims." This proclamation stopped the burning of churches and the killing of Christians.

Let us not forget that in the Church we have Judases whose mission is sabotage and to kill spiritual ministers. A story is told of a Baptist minister who was spirit filled and had developed his parish spiritually. This didn't please the Judases in his parish and they convinced the board and had the minister fired. Within a short time, the minister was called to a bigger parish which gave him a bigger stipend. In the same month when the minister was exalted, one Judas suffered a heart attached and died, another Judas became blind and the third Judas lost his job.

Apparently, Padre Penda was ministering in the same town as a Chaplain and lecturer of Kiswahili in the University. He brought with him the impartation from Nakuru, which was the most ecumenical city in the world. In this town, the priest was perceived as a minister to the community rather than a possession of a particular clique. He initiated several programs which included a KWANZA celebration, a Bible study for all the people of God, and a mission to low income families. He started the PRESS ON program for the children from these families. He also launched a monthly program known as Canterbury, which was a celebration of all cultures represented in the University. During this monthly program, a particular people prepared their traditional food and wore their country attire. The Nigerians would bring Fufu and wear their ethnic dress and play their music. The Jamaican would prepare a chicken in such a way that you will think that it has been imported from Jamaica.

Penda was one of the main speakers during the annual International Week and on March 8, 1995, he was awarded the certificate of recognition which read: "Certificate of recognition and appreciation presented … in recognition and appreciation of your outstanding contribution in promoting international awareness and cultural diversity in the University.

Whenever he was going for a vacation in Kenya, Penda took a team of missioners and they ministered to the clergy in four Anglican Dioceses and students in at least four public high schools. The missioners received more than what they imparted and when they came back, did great work in building up the Kingdom of God far beyond their denominational boundaries.

These activities infuriated the chairman of the small denominational congregation (whom we will call Munjuga) which had called Penda. He maligned Penda and accused him of being too ecumenical. The more Penda initiated spiritual and interdenominational activities, the greater was the fight from Munjuga, who, though a lead of a congregation, was a Mason. In the author's opinion, for the Mason, three things are the ideal-sexual immorality, money and power. This was contrary to the Holy Spirit. What will the Dynamic Power of the Holy Spirit do?

On one occasion, Penda was driving home from the Denominational Convention. He was tired and almost worn out. He then asked God, "How long will you let this man sabotage your mission? This is not my mission. It is your mission." Reaching home, the very first call came from Munjuga's wife reporting that her husband is dead. Before he died he had informed his family that he would not like Penda to perform his funeral service. However, it has to be done by a former priest whom Mumjuga had induced to be fired. This white priest gave an unusual homily. He talked to Munjuga in the casket saying, "Munjuga, you have wrestled with power in the church and university; you are now going to face Him who has all power."

So, beloved, though you may be going through what the Baptist minister and Padre Penda went through, remember that God is in control and has your best interest at heart. Remember what the word of God says: The Spirit himself testifies with our spirit that we are God's children. Now if we are children, then we are heirs- heirs of God and co-heirs with Christ, if we indeed share in his **suffering** in order that we may also share in his glory. Romans 8: 15-17.

CHAPTER FIVE

SIGNS AND WONDERS

Luke reports: "The apostles performed many signs and wonders among the people". Acts 15:12. The third person of Trinity performs many signs and wonders in winning people for Christ, deliverance, provision, and destroying so as to make it holy. These signs are visible. The Bible tells us: "crowds also gathered from the towns around Jerusalem, bringing their sick and those tormented by impure spirits, and all of them were healed." Acts 5:16. Signs and wonders are not for self-glorification. Synoptic Gospels reports that most of the time when Jesus healed he told the person that he has healed not to tell anybody.

Let start with wonders in provision. It has been said that God does not give vision without provision, but there's always a problem between the vision and provision. God allows this so as to show signs and wonders. For instance, Padre Penda ministered faithfully and prophetically to a traditional Church which was comprised of professionals. But he had a vision of reaching out to the Sudanese and other new immigrants, most of who had low income with lesser or no education. Eventually he was kicked out by the traditional church and evicted from the parish house. God showed him wonders. He needed to purchase a house, but he had no money. One time, when he was visiting with a friend, the man gave him $5000 for the down payment and another gave him, $3000. Another miracle happened when he sent an empty envelope to a friend. He was so tired and exhausted when he was sending the letter to his friend that he forgot to insert the letter into the envelope. A few days later he got a call from the friend who asked, "Penda: why did you send me an empty envelope?" Penda responded, "I am so sorry. I will send you another one and invite you for supper." So, Penda and his wife and his friends had supper in a restaurant. After enjoying the meal, Penda was given the ticket. His friends grumbled the ticket and said, "Your money is no good here." He then told the waiter, "Clear the table; we have serious business." He then wrote Penda a Check for $2000. Miraculously, in the year that Penda was evicted from the Parish house, God provided him with five properties, four of which were rental properties. This was very much like the Baptist minister who was fired for being prophetic and eventually he got a bigger parish and the three Judases lost much – life, sight and job.

So, my friend, if you are being afflicted for being faithful, believe that God will come at the right time for you. His promise is to never leave you nor forsake you. Deuteronomy 31:6, Deuteronomy 31:8, Joshua 1:5, 1 Kings 8:57, 1 Chronicles 28:20, Psalms 37:28, Psalms 94:14, Isaiah 41:17, Isaiah 42:16, and Hebrews 13:5.

If you are a priest killer, repent and turn to God. This is the message from the Risen Lord, "Look, I am coming soon! My reward is with me, and I will give to each person according to what they have done. I am the Alpha and the Omega, the First and the Last, the Beginning and the End." Revelation 22:12.

As we have seen, the Prophet's reward includes suffering and glorification. Glorification takes place when we are on the mountain interceding for the people of God. Jesus was transfigured when he was on the mountain. Let us hear about Moses.

CHAPTER SIX

THE RADIANCE OF THE HOLY SPIRIT

When Moses was on the Mountain, he beseeched God to reveal Himself to him. He prayed: "Lord, you have been telling me, 'lead my people.' But you have let me know who you will send with me. You have said: "you have found favor with me, teach me your way so I may know you and continue to find favor with you. Remember this nation is your people." The Lord replied, my Presence will go with you, and I will give you rest." Then Moses asked God: "show me your glory." God assured Moses that He will be with him and He showed Moses His glory. Then the Bible tells us: "When Moses came down from Mount Sinai with two tablet of the covenant law in his hands, he was not aware that his face was radiant because he has spoken with Lord. When Aaron and all Israelites saw Moses, his face was radiant, and they were afraid to come near him" Exodus 34:29-30. Interestingly, the Psalmist speaks of this radiation and how it overcomes fear and shame. He says: "I sought the Lord, and he answered me. He delivered me from all my fears. Those who look to him are **radiant**, their faces are never covered with shame." Psalm 34:4-5 According to this Psalm, those who radiated are seeing and tasting the Lord. They may have many troubles, but the Lord will deliver them from all their afflictions. They are guarded by the angel of the Lord. And thus, instead of fear, they exalt and glorify the Lord. The promise in this psalm is for those who are radiating, "The Lord will rescue his servants; no one who take refuge in him will be condemned." Psalm 34: 22.

Let us go back to Padre Penda who has now ministered to and with many nations. Over the years, he has been surprised by so many people who have asked him, "Are you a preacher?" And also by strangers saying to him, "You are a preacher". The very first person to tell him that his face was radiating was his mother when he was seventeen. That same year, Penda was walking home and met a lady who stated to him, "You look like a man of God." He was astonished to get similar comments from people of different races in the USA. At one time, it happened when he was ministering in the Hospital. He was descending from the second floor when he saw three African American women talking and looking at him. Arriving where they were, one lady said, "We are talking about you." He asked her, "What are you saying?" She said: "Look at me!" I don't have my glasses and I am near sighted; but when you were up there, I told my friends, that is a man of God." "How did you know?" asked Padre Penda. "A light on the hill cannot be hid." responded the lady. [3]

Penda was dumbfounded when he attended Texas. open air drama performed at Palo Duro Canyon State Park near Canyon, Texas. He had dressed as a cowboy with cowboy- belt and -hat. He wore no religious symbol. Before the drama, he visited with people. He was not preaching. But a man who was dressed as a clown asked him: "What do you do for living?" I am a Bishop." responded Penda. The clown said, "Stand here." Penda don't know what the man was planning to do with him. But, as people were coming he would approach them and say, "Look at this

---

[3] "You are the light of the world. A town built on a hill cannot be hidden. Matthew 5:14.

man and tell me what he does for living." The first person challenged, a white lady, looked at Penda and said, "This man is a preacher."

Another episode took place on a Monday, Penda's day off. On this day, he does not do religious symbols. On the day in question, he went to the "food court" in West Gate Mall[4] and ordered a glass of lemon juice. He sat down sipping juice as he read about the Deity of Christ from Free Grace booklet. As he was reading, someone touched his hand. He was a white man who asked, "Are you a pastor?" "Yes I am. How did you know?" Penda asked. "I am also a Pastor of Salvation Army." he explained. They then had a short visit before bidding each other goodbye.

Another incident took place when Penda was on a flight sitting next to a Mexican lady. She greeted Penda with the affirmation, "You are a preacher." "How did you know?" Penda queried. She answered, "I see you with a religious book." Penda was reading Heaven by Dr. Joseph Okello. Then Penda asked whether she has committed herself to Christ. She told him that she is a Catholic and that the short coming of her church is that they discouraged the member from reading the Bible and interacting with other Christians. But what was reassuring being that the lady, though a Roman Catholic and uncomfortable with her lack of Bible study, was able to see the radiating presence of the Holy Spirit in Padre Penda.

These illustrations suffice to show that when the Spirit of Him who claimed to be the light of the world is in us, people can see that light in us. Interestingly, the person who planted the seed of the Gospel was our Headmaster, Bernard Mwangi, when I was fourteen. I don't remember him preaching to us. But I remember that one time he came to the class and gave each one of us three canes.[5] Then the following day he

---

[4] In Amarillo, Texas.

[5] That is, each was hit with a cane three times, usually done as punishment.

apologized. I had never heard any African authority figure apologizing. So, after that time I started paying more attention to him, and I could see his face glowing with peace. The events inspired my song. I would sing, "One day, I will commit myself to Christ." The seed which Bernard planted germinated two years later.

I would like to remind you once again what the Risen Lord says. "I am the vine; you are the branches. If you remain in me and I in you, you will bear much fruit; apart from me, you can do nothing." John 15:5. We bear much fruit by going far beyond the call of duty. Let us here more about what Padre Penda does.

CHAPTER SEVEN

SUFFERING AND GLORIFICATION

DID YOU NOTE THAT suffering is what we have to go through if we are co-heirs with Christ? Did Jesus promise that our blessing include suffering? The very word witness in the great promise is the same word with martyr – someone who says, "No matter what you will do with my body, as long as I have breath in my mouth I will not stop proclaiming Jesus and Lord." So, unlike Prosperity Gospel preachers, Jesus didn't promise glory without the cross. For the man of the Spirit, glorification may be followed by suffering and, then, after suffering there is glorification. In case of our Lord, glorification preceded the desert experience. Luke reports,

> "When all the people were being baptized, Jesus was baptized too. And as he was praying the heaven was open and the Holy Spirit descended on him like a dove. And a voice came from heaven: "you are my son, whom I love, with whom I am well pleased."

Luke 3:21-22. After the glorification, Luke relates that,

> "Jesus, full of the Holy Spirit, return from Jordan and was led by the Spirit in the desert, where for forty days he was tempted by the devil. He ate nothing during those days, and at the end of them he was **hungry**." Luke 4:1-2.

For a man of Spirit, the wilderness experience is not a onetime deal. It is a recurring experience. It lasts forty[6] days which can be a period of two weeks, two months or three years. See Dr John Githiga : *FROM VICTORY TO VICTORY* and *MINISTRY TO ALL NATIONS* at www.drjohngithiga.com

One of the creatures in the desert is the devil, who is one of the craftiest beasts.. Not only does he know the weapon which he will use to inflict pain, he is shrewd in selecting the animal that will use the weapon. Note that in case of Jesus, he used Judas, one of his disciples with whom he has entrusted the useful ministry of treasurer. Judas was also a family name. The name Jude (the name of a brother of Jesus who wrote the *Epistle of Jude*) is the same. King David, a man after God's own heart, was hunted by his father-in-law. Absalom, his most handsome boy, wanted to overturn the government of his father. Satan will use the members of your family or those people whom you have embraced in your heart to hurt you.

Padre Penda had several of these humiliating experiences. One episode occurred when he visited, St Nicholas's Church which he planted in 1970s. The church had grown and birthed three other parishes. It is located in the children's home which Penda founded. So, Penda had a habit of taking missioners to the home and they gave a big donation. He had also included the home in his will. With the busy trip schedule, which included several Clergy Conferences, he had only one Sunday before he had to return to USA. He was also with the only woman

---

[6] The number '40' appears over 150 times in the Bible and is associated with testing or trial.

bishop in ANCCI. So, on Saturday he visited with the Priest in charge and informed him that they are in the town and would like to minister at St Nicholas's. He agreed. But on Sunday upon arriving at the church, they were led to an officer by the Priest who told them that a word has come from the Bishop stating that they are not allowed to preach since they didn't follow protocol. They can sit in the congregation and greet people during the announcements. So, during the announcements, the lady bishop took one minute and greeted the congregation. Then Penda stood and quickly said, "Let me give a short story of this church. In 1970s there was a young man who lived in Christ. And in obedience to Christ he planted this church. So, I want to leave you with the word of Jesus[7], "I am the vine. You are the branches. If a man remains in me and I in him, he will bear much fruit; apart from me you can do nothing." As he was finishing this sentence the priest handed note to him advising, "time to sit down."

What would hurt Penda the most was that the Bishop who issued the command was a member of his youth group. Moreover, when he was planting the church, he was accused to his bishop that he had started a church which was not Anglican. However, the mother church was claiming all the offering. So, the money was Anglican, but the congregation was not Anglican. However, Penda had no anger because he knows that rejection was a part of our calling: He remembered what the Apostle John wrote about Jesus, "He came to what was his own but his own did not receive him." John 1:11.

Just as the angels who ministered to Jesus[8], Penda and his Bishop were ministered by a Messianic Congregation, who they visited after the rejection at St. Nicholas. They were received by and the Bishop and were asked to preach. In the same evening, they were visited by St. Nicholas'

---

[7] John 15:5.
[8] Matthew 4:11, Mark1:13, Luke 22:43, and Hebrews 1:14.

Harmony, a musical group from the same congregation which rejected them in the morning. Their music was both entertaining and uplifting.

Satan does not leave us alone until our final glorification. He comes at an opportune time. Luke tells us, "When the devil finishes all this tempting, he left him until an opportune time." Luke 4:13. He found such an opportunity when Padre Penda was attending the Memorial for his mother who was known as Wagatungu. The name has double meaning -- mother of Gatungu (Gatungu being Penda's name) and daughter of Gatungu. Penda's community is both patrilineal and matrilineal and for that reason when the community selected that name for her it was a great honor to Penda. At the Memorial, the family, which is comprised of a Canon, Rural Dean and Diocesan Bishop, gathered together for the division of labor. They asked Penda to be the preacher. Before they entered the Church, the Diocesan Bishop, who had previously said that he would not be available, popped in. Penda's brother Bishop told the Diocesan bishop that the family had decided that Penda will be the preacher. The Bishop responded, "He cannot preach because this is the time that I give directives in my diocese." Penda felt a sharp pain in his umbilical cord, but quickly heard a whisper of his mom saying, "Wichekehie." It means shrink yourself and edge through. So, with humility and low voice, he said to the Diocesan Bishop, "But I would like to give tribute to my mother." "Tribute, yes, but sermon no!" said the Diocesan Bishop. Entering the church Penda was thrilled to see that the church was filled to the brim. There were a good number of priests who had been his seminary students. Others had come from his Bishop-brother's Diocese. Still others came from the parish of his brother, the Canon and his Nephew, the Rural Dean. All the family members and their friends were there. Penda who was first on the program took his Bible with him to the podium. The Diocesan Bishop whispered to Penda's brother Bishop, "Did I not tell him not to preach? Now he is taking the Bible with him." Penda preached for 30 minutes and then asked his wife to give the tribute. His wife, who is very tactful, asked the key members of the family to each give short tribute and then she concluded with her tribute. Finally, the Diocesan Bishop was asked to give his directives. His message was directed to Penda and was amusing. He declared that, "When you come; do not leave all the money in your brother's Diocese. You much bring some money to this Diocese." After the service, when they were exiting. Penda quickly realized that there was a spot where his wife would trip and fall as she had fallen several times because of the jetlag. So, he held her hand. The Diocesan Bishop who was super critical to Penda commented, "Here we do not hold women's hand in public." "So you let them fall?" responded Penda's wife. "I am just kidding." responded the Bishop. To this end, it is evident that power without the authority is dangerous. It reduced the person to what psychoanalysis terms as: "his majesty the baby."[9]

As St. Paul wrote,

> No temptation[a] has overtaken you except what is common to mankind. And God is faithful; he will not let you be tempted[b] beyond what you can bear. But when you are tempted,[c] he will also provide a way out so that you can endure it.1 Corinthian 10:13.

What happened to Penda is typical what had happened to so many men and women in diaspora. For instance, a Pastor who is a Kenyan missionary in Bahama was refused permission to preach at the funeral of his mother by a parish priest who claimed, "This is my parish and so I am the preacher." There is a time when we must do what the Spirit tells us. To the church leaders in Jerusalem, do realize that funeral and memorials are family affairs! More importantly, it is the time to comfort and console the family. It is not the time for demonstrating your power. If you are looking for eternal reward, serve in the Spirit of Christ who teaches, "You know that those who are regarded as rulers of the Gentiles

---

[9] A phrase first used by Sigmund Freud. The expression refers to childish traits seen in people who have reached adulthood without emotional maturity

lord it over them, and their high officials exercise authority over them. Not so with you. Instead, whoever wants to become great among you must be your servant and whoever wants to be first must be a slave of all. Mark 10: 42-44.

The major lesson which we learn from these stories is that if we abide in Christ, we will always bear fruits. And no human being can separate us from our fruits. The fruits which we bear remain forever. So, if you plant in tear, you will harvest with joy. You will have several desert experiences. But whatever problem you face, remember, Jesus went to the desert full of the Holy Spirit and came out of the desert full of the Holy Spirit. So, stay firmly connected with the Holy Spirit. Whatever you are going through, do not lose the joy of the Holy Spirit. Remember, after performing many signs and wonders, the apostles provoked the jealousy of the religious leaders, were arrested and brought to the Sanhedrin, who flogged them and told them to never speak of the name Jesus. What was their reaction? The Bible tells us: The apostles left the Sanhedrin, rejoicing because they had been counted worthy of suffering disgrace for the Name. Day after day, in the temple courts and from house to house, they never stopped teaching and proclaiming the good news that Jesus is the Messiah." Acts 5:41-42.

Let us hear more about the Spirit in Padre Penda.

CHAPTER EIGHT

THE HOLY SPIRIT IN PADRE PENDA

As noted, Penda lives in Nakuru Boys' Centre where he rehabilitates and cares for the troubled boys. He loves them and identifies himself with them. When going to the dumpsite to persuade them to come to the Centre, he wears patched clothes. Because of his relationship with the "children of the dustbins," he is addressed by Nakuru children as the "dumpster." Whenever they see him they sing for him:

> Mapipa (The dustbin)
> Mapipa
> Mapipa

This song hurts him. However, because of his love, humility and self-control he does not retaliate. He has won the affection of many parking boys.[10] They regard him as the faithful "Field Marshall" of their many gang-groups which they call "battalions". Due to his love and goodness, Penda has helped many boys to stop inhaling petrol, smoking opium, and robbing people in

---

[10] Parking boys are unsupervised, though not necessarily orphaned, who roam the streets of towns in Kenya.

the shops and streets. Although they tell Padre Penda stories of how they steal, they have never stolen anything from Penda – not even a cent.

Penda and his wife had many rewarding and challenging episodes. One humorous incident was a visit of four boys in their house. One of the boys was crying, claiming that he was beaten by one of the four boys. Penda and Madam wondered how the accused could come together with the accuser. So instead of solving the case immediately, Madam prepared tea for them. Penda told them stories. They seemed to enjoy evening of parenting. Eventually the boys revealed their secret, "We really didn't have problem with each other. We wanted to be with you. This this is why we faked the fight." These boys who live on the street coveted the presence of a parent figure. Penda discovered that most of their problems were caused by environmental problems. Most of them came from single parent families who were selling the only commodity of value they had -- sex. During the story telling most of them confirmed that prostitution was the major reason why they had to go to street. One boy said during the story-telling session, "Whenever a customer came, even if it was mid-night, we had to get out. And because of this problem, I decided to join the gangs on the street."

Penda witnessed a harsh situation. He knew a boy named Babu whose home was only two miles from the Centre. During the holidays, he preferred to stay in the Centre. On one occasion Penda decided to take Babu to his home. He didn't have a mother, but did have two sisters who were supposed to take care of him. Entering the house, they found the two sisters and a five-year-old girl. The only seat which was available was the bed. So, Penda was welcomed to seat on the bed. After little talk, Babu and one sister left. Then the five-year-old told Penda, "Now we are going out and we are going to leave both of you." Suddenly, Penda noticed a snake. So, he told the little girl, "I am also leaving with you." Penda left and asked Babu to join him on the motor cycle and they went back to the Centre.

So, the more Penda ministered to the children, the more he realized that troubled homes and family lives were the major causes of their problems.

CHAPTER NINE

PASTRORAL SEMINAR IN NAKURU HIGH

In spite of his busy program at the Centre, street, and dumpsite, Padre Penda leads a pastoral seminar at Nakuru High. He goes there every Friday and spends an hour with fifty students. The majority of youngsters take a great interest in Padre. They like the way he leads a discussion.

It is now Friday morning. Padre Penda is waking up at 5 a.m. to have a devotion which included Bible reading and praying in Spirit for forty-five minutes. This time he is being more inspired by the Holy Spirit than ever. He is praying to God to help him to be more loving and patient.

At 7:30 a.m. Padre Penda is on his motor cycle. He is driving to Nakuru High. He is passing through Kamathi Estate. Children are singing for him:

> Mapipa (dumpster)
> Mapipa
> Mapipa

Mapipa
Mapipa
Mapipa
Mapipa
Mapipa

Penda is being hurt: However, he is praying to the Lord to help him to forgive them:

> Lord, forgive them
> They are your children
> Help me to love them more and more.

Padre Penda is accelerating his scooter. He remembers that forbearance is one of the fruits of the Spirit. He believes that the Holy Spirit will help him to forbear the children who were mocking him. After forgiving these children Padre Penda is filled with the peace of the Holy Spirit which passes all understanding. He is now near Nakuru State Lodge. He is driving towards Nairobi. The day is very bright. Every leaf is decorated by dew. The glittering of the dew is enhancing his joy. Padre Penda is full of the joy of the Holy Spirit. The joy is increasing as he remembers Paul's words:

> Rejoice in the Lord always,
> again I will say Rejoice.

Finally, Padre Penda is at Nakuru High. The youngsters are eagerly waiting for him. He is in the class. He stands to give the opening remarks. After speaking for a short time James, one of the students, dashes in from outside. He shouts to Padre Penda:

James:	By what authority are you teaching these things?
Padre:	By the authority of Christ.
James:	How can someone who is not born again dare to stand before the believers?
Padre:	What do you mean by being born again?

James:	I mean how can someone who is not Spirit-filled teach those who are filled with the Holy Spirit?
Padre:	Do you mean that I do not have the Spirit of God?
James:	How can someone who does not speak in tongues claim to have the Holy Spirit? We do not even need your theology.
Padre:	What do you mean by theology?
James:	God-made-man.

To stop James from taking over the seminar, Padre Penda orders him to sit down and see him after the seminar. After the class, Padre Penda spends twenty minutes with James. Padre Penda discovers that the problem with James is the question of "speaking in tongues." He does not believe that Padre Penda is born again because he thinks that Penda does not speak in tongues. James does not understand the difference between the gifts of the Holy Spirit and the fruits of the Holy Spirit. He also knows very little about the work of the Sprit. Let us discuss the work, the gifts, and the fruits of the Holy Spirit.

CHAPTER TEN

THE WORK OF THE HOLY SPIRIT

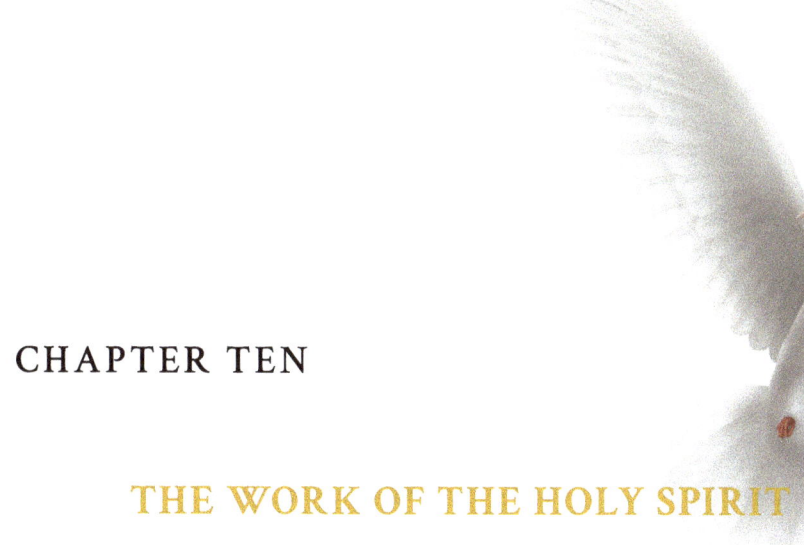

THE KIKUYU INITIATION INCLUDES a very important person known as Mutiiri. Mutiiri is like a sponsor or a godparent. A day prior to initiation, he prepares and advises the initiate. During the initiation, Mutiiri sits or stands behind the initiate in order to support him.

In this frightening moment, Mutiiri acts as the only source of comfort and encouragement. He helps the initiate to relax as he waits for the frightening circumciser.

After the initiation, Mutiiri helps the initiate to walk home or to the place of seclusion. During the seclusion, he nurses and teaches the initiate all the secrets of the tribe. After the seclusion, Mutiiri becomes the supreme adviser to that individual.

The Spirit of God, like Mutiiri, is our supporter and helper during our life crisis. He is a dynamic presence, counsellor, comforter, advocate, reconciler and defender. He gives us wisdom, understanding, knowledge and power. While the Sprit is always with us, his dynamic presence is felt and realized in a greater capacity during our developmental and situational crises or the dark night of the soul. The Holy Spirit, like Mutiiri, does not avert pain, but helps us to confront pain with hope and courage. If we listen to and obey the Holy Spirit during our critical moments, we come out with only a minimum of damage but with a maximum of profit. We gain from crisis.

As the Bible indicates, the Sprit equipped the Israelites for service and imparted skill to their craftsmen (Exodus 31:3) and gave wisdom to their judges and Kings (Judges 3:10). He also gave physical power to their deliverers. He inspired the prophets and helped them to predict the permanent indwelling of the Holy Spirit in the Christian community. The same Spirit empowered Jesus during all his turning points. He operated during Mary's conception of Jesus. As we confess in the Nicene Creed:

> "For us men and for our salvation
> he came down from heaven;
> by the power of the Holy Spirit
> He became incarnate from the Virgin Mary, and was made man."

Then Mary conceived through the power of the Holy Spirit (Luke 1:35). The Spirit was present during Jesus' birth (Luke 2:25-7), his baptism (Mathew 3:18), his temptation and entry into the ministry (Luke 4:14), his exorcising of the evil spirit and commissioning of the disciples (Matthew 28:19).

As with Jesus, the Holy Spirit was felt in a special way during the developmental stages of the church. He came mightily during the birth of the Church. The writer of the Book of Acts says, "When the day of Pentecost had come they were all together in one place. And suddenly, a sound came from heaven like the rush of a mighty wind, and it filled all the house where they were sitting… And they were filled with the Holy Spirit. (Acts 2:1-4). In addition, the Holy Spirit operated during the sending out of the missionaries and guided the decisions of the first Church Council.

In the Gospel of John, the Holy Spirit is depicted as an advocate, comforter, counsellor, and helper. The disciples experienced him as dynamic presence. They believed, as the Lord has promised them, that he will remain with them forever. The Spirit is only known and realized by disciples. The world can neither see nor know Him. Like Mutiiri, the Spirit guides the disciples into all truth, "When the Spirit comes, he will guide you into all truth." John 16:13. The work of the Holy Spirit is therefore to move us from our knowing and push us to the edge of our knowing. He challenges us to move from "a simple Gospel" to the mystery of life. He challenges us to transcend ourselves and listen to He-who-lives-beyond us. The Spirit does not call us to glorify ourselves like James who thought of himself as being more "born again" than Padre Penda. He calls us to exalt Christ. He develops and clarifies the teaching of Jesus. He directs our attention to God the Son and God the Father.

Since He proceeds from the father and the Son he has all the substance of the Triune God. To receive the Spirit is to receive the Father and Son. However, the Holy Spirit can be distinguished from the Father who sends Him, and from the Son in whose name He is sent, but the three cannot be separated. If the Spirit is present, the Son and the Father are present as well.

When the Spirit of God comes into our lives, he gives us his gifts. The gifts are used to maintain the body of Christ – the church.

CHAPTER ELEVEN

THE GIFTS OF THE HOLY SPIRIT

We can use African traditional society to illustrate the gifts of the Holy Spirit. Customarily, African communities are organized by various specialists. We have kings, chiefs, priests, diviners, herbalists, prophets, rainmakers, hunters, smiths, and so on. Each specialist plays his or her role and uses symbols that are related to the office. No specialist is expected to play all the roles. Similarly, the spirit gives us a variety of gifts. These gifts include wisdom, knowledge, faith, healing, working of miracles, prophecy, discernment, speaking in tongues, interpretation of tongues, administration, and many others. None of these gifts is superior or inferior to the others. None of these gifts is compulsory for all believers. Not all members of the Church are expected to be healers or speakers of tongues. We are not all expected to be bishops or teachers. These gifts are not for self-glorification but "for the common good." Thus, James was wrong in regarding himself more "Christian" than Padre Penda because the former speaks in tongues. He did not realize that Padre Penda had many gifts of the Holy Spirit such as administrating, teaching, and preaching, including speaking in tongue.

Moreover, there is a need to test the Spirit. Ecstatic speech is not the audible proof that a person is spirit-filled. Furthermore, ecstasy is not exclusively Christian. For instance, the Kikuyu initiation dances were marked with ecstasy. On the other hand, the orderliness of worship which is devoid of emotion, is also not the proof of the existence of the Holy Spirit. Those Christians who condemn all emotion and feeling are not better than those who over emphasize the gift of the speaking in tongues. It is not Biblical to totally rule out speaking in tongue in Church. The Bible says this about the day of Pentecost, "They were all filled with the Holy Spirit and began to speak in other languages." Acts 2:1-13. Those who stand at either extreme position demonstrates a lack of understanding of the fruits of the Holy Spirit. While we are not expected to have all the gifts of the Spirit, we are expected to have all the fruits of the Holy Spirit.

CHAPTER TWELVE

THE FRUIT OF THE HOLY SPIRIT

But the fruit of the spirit is love, joy, peace, patience, kindness, goodness, faithfulness, self-control, against such there is no law.
— Galatian 5:19

1. Love

As we have seen, Padre Penda demonstrated the love of God in his love for the street boys. Although these boys were rejected by the society, Padre loved them and cared for them as his children or younger brothers. This love shows that Padre is born again. The writer of the first Epistle of John says, "Let us love one another for God is love, and he who loves is born of God and knows God. He who does not love does not know God; for God is love." 1 John 4:7-8. Our godliness is measured by our love for our fellow men.

Love is a fruit of the Holy Spirit. When our lives are filled with the Spirit we demonstrate brother- and sisterly love. We welcome and entertain our neighbors. We love them dearly. We accept them as they are. We are pleased and contented with them in spite of their weaknesses. To have the love of the Holy Spirit means to have a warm feeling towards other persons. This results in our winning them to us as they won us to themselves.

Love means forgiving. Jesus showed a forgiving love on the cross. He prayed for those who were torturing him: "Father forgive them; for they do not know what they do." Luke 23:34. The love of the Holy Spirit reconciles us to one another. It also gives us humility and courage to serve. True love which comes from the Spirit means renunciation of our lust and sin. Like Padre Penda, the love of the Spirit may lead us to give up some of our rights and power. A loving and a serving Christian, is also a joyous person.

2.   Joy

Joy is another fruit of the Holy Spirit. This fruit is seen in the person of Padre Penda. For when he was insulted by Nakuru children as he was going to Nakuru High, he did not allow himself to be overwhelmed with anger. He remembered that the joy of the Spirit is his strength. His motto was: "rejoice in the Lord always."

Interestingly, Padre Penda had a chance of going to the United States to study for a Master of Divinity Degree. He was a student in the University of the Mountain. While he was there he used the joy of the Spirit as one of the weapons to fight against daily confusion. If he made a mistake, he laughed at himself and let it go.

However, Padre Penda was surprised to learn that some Americans regarded joy as repression and anger as the feeling of the feelings. They argue, "You cannot know someone unless you have seen his anger."

On one occasion, he was very confused when he was asked the following questions by an instructor playing the role of a psychiatrist, "Penda, do you ever get angry" How many times have you been angry since you came here to the Mountain? What do you do with your anger?" Eventually, when Padre Penda was doing clinical Pastoral Education, he became aware that anger was necessary if he was to get his certificate. He then decided to play their game. During the peer group and supervisory meeting, he used a Kikuyu initiation philosophy of confrontation. He put on the mask of anger. Nevertheless, this mask was weakened by his love for the peers, supervisor, and the patients. For this reason, he did not succeed in being as angry as he was supposed to be. The following were the comments from his peer group:

From a twenty-nine-year-old Lutheran white women seminarian:

> Being me, I've a problem of relating with all my peers, and so it should not come as shock that Penda presented his own set of difficulties. I like Penda from the very beginning, he's a very likable fellow. I have appreciated his warmth and cheerfulness, but I still don't know if he has appreciated my anger since he has not let me appreciate his.

From a twenty-five-year-old Lutheran white male seminarian:

> Penda is a very easy person to establish rapport with. He is very friendly and pastoral. He is non-threatening, non-challenging and non-aggressive. I am sure that he is the layman's image of what a pastor ought to be: educated, gentle, kind, touched by God in a special way. Sometimes I resent that image. It exalts Christianity at the cost of humanity.

According to the seminarians, Padre Penda's weakest point is lack of anger. In their eyes, to be a "good leader" one must have the ability to be angry towards others. The ideal Pastor is one who can be aggressive. Here we may predict that if the god-of-anger succeeds in dominating the ministry in America, in this generation, he will be repudiated by the next generation. Anger is the opposite of joy. It is not the most desirable feeling, for it has neither psychological nor spiritual reward. It does not build the family. Anger toward each other, whether caused by children, money, or power struggle, is the major cause of family tension and marriage breakdown. Anger is a kind of spiritual disease which debilitates us just as a physical disease would. It breaks down love relationships, interferes with communication, leads to guilt and depression, and generally just gets in our way. As we say in Swahili: *Hasira hasara* [Anger is a loss].

Nevertheless, we are not rejecting the fact that anger is one of our human feelings. We are not saying that clergymen and Christians cannot get angry. Yet, we are rejecting a psychological "heresy" which maintains that anger is the best means of interpersonal relationships. We are refusing the idea that the ideal person is the one who is led by his or her feelings. My strong belief is: I think; therefore, I feel.

Christian joy however, is more than "feeling good." It is a precious quality of life which springs from the Holy Spirit. It also comes from the Gospel of Christ: "For behold, I bring you good news of a great joy which will come to all people." Luke 2:20. This joy is fueled by faith and prayer and meditation. The promise of Christ to the believers is: "ask and you will receive that your joy may be full." John 16:24. The joy of the Spirit is kept burning by service to others. When we have faithfully served, there is a real joy at the end of the day. Furthermore, the word of Christ gives us joy: He says: "these things I have spoken to you, that my joy may be in you and that your joy may be full." John 15:11. The joy of the Spirit is therefore beyond our expression. It is more than just being humorous. It is not repression; it is the quality of life which flows from God himself. It does not depend on good happenings. With the Spirit in our hearts we can smile at the storm. This joy is healthy and has a healing power. It wells from the peace of God which passes all understanding.

3. Peace

Now we come to peace. In the Old Testament, peace means completeness, wholeness and health. It is used for an individual and communal wholeness which includes material and spiritual blessings.

It denotes the nation's political, economic and military prosperity. A peaceful man is also expected to have a good sleep and a blessed long-life.

While the New Testament does not ignore the notion of political and economic prosperity, it uses the word peace in a deeper and spiritual way. Peace, as a fruit of the Holy Spirit, comes from God and is the sign of His presence. This peace can be felt in the absence of political and economic prosperity and military protection. We can be filled with this peace even when we are being persecuted.

This fruit can be illustrated by the experience of Samuel Muhoro and his wife Sara. It was a dark and cold night while the couple was in deep sleep in their home in Kiruri. At midnight, the persecutors came with a huge log and broke down the door. Sara awoke immediately. But before she woke her husband, the gang was standing beside the bed. They then tried to force Samuel and his wife to recant Christ by cutting the former like a piece of wood with large knives. The blood was pouring out like water from his face and shoulder. He could not see properly since the blood had blinded his eyes. While Sara was watching this horrible drama, she was filled with an extraordinary peace of the Holy Spirit. She then gave a big smile. The persecutors, astonished at Sara's peace and joy, stopped killing Samuel and said to Sara, "Why are you smiling at us? Don't you know that we are murderers?" "I know. But God loves you." Sara responded. They then cut her small finger. But in spite of pain she remained calm. The peace of the Holy Spirit averted the gang's plan of killing the couple. But, the would-be murders took all the blankets.

When they were leaving, Sara said to them peacefully and jokingly, "Folks! Don't forget that we have children. Don't take all the blankets." Then the murderers turned to her and threw some of the blankets to her. A gang member also threw down the cassock of Rev Samuel and said, "Be praying for us." Samuel, who survived to tell the story, said, "Sara and I had peace in our hearts. What amazed us and made us praise God, was that all the time we were being chopped we did not feel pain at all, nor did we show any sign of grief or despair." I believe this is what the New Testament means by peace. It is the calmness of the inner life which keeps us hopeful in a hopeless situation.

This peace reconciles man to God. As Paul says, "In Christ God was reconciling the world to himself, not counting their trespasses against them, but entrusting to us the message of reconciliation." II Corinthians 5:19. This fruit of the Sprit reconciles man with man, and man with the rest of creation. It helps us to love the world and care for God's creation. This peace, which is born out of and nurtured by faith, gives calmness and serenity of mind. It is the means and end to Christian life. It keeps our hearts and minds in Christ Jesus, who says: "Peace I leave with you; my peace I give to you; not as the world gives do I give to you. Let not your heart be troubled neither let them be afraid." John 13:27.

4. **Forbearance**

Although other fruits of the Spirit are related to willingness to forgive injuries, this quality is especially concerned with the acceptance of those who are not really acceptable. This gift is evident in the person of Padre Penda who loved "the dustbin boys" (watoto wa mapipa) and identified himself with them. He loved them although they had a lot of problems in responding to his love.

Forbearance means to love the unlovable. Even in conflict it will give consideration to the welfare of the cause that the forbearing person does not favor. Jomo Kenyatta, the first President of Kenya, is one of our modern examples. He was imprisoned by the British and suffered hunger and other ordeals in prison. But, when he was released and asked, "Now that the Government is in your hands, what will you do with the Britons?", he forbearingly answered, "We are going to forgive them and show them by our love that we are better than them." Jomo Kenyatta forbore the Britons who tortured him for eight years, labeling him communist and regarding him as a person who is intended to lead the country into darkness. Dr. Martin Luther King, a black American Pastor, is another example. Dr. King, while he spoke for the American Blacks, identified with the oppressed wherever they might be and strove to establish human dignity for everyone. He insisted that the plan for liberation must be carried forward without violence. He spoke as strongly for the right of the oppressed white population as for those of the Blacks. He was also aware that his opponents were as much in bondage to their past as were the people whom he sought to help.

Thus, this quality of the Holy Spirit helps us to forbear the un-forbear-able. It also helps us to embrace those who unconsciously remind us of all the evil which resides in us. By embracing them, we also embrace that part of us which we do not like.

5. Kindness

Kindness is another fruit of the Holy Spirit. The original word which Paul uses also means gentleness and generosity. Generosity in this sense is far more than a matter of being generous with money. One can be gentle, kind and generous even when he has no money for Harambee.[11] It is a quality that can be found in people with no money to give, beginning perhaps with Peter when he declared that he had no silver or gold but undertook to give what he did have. Acts 3:6. As a fruit of the Spirit the only way really to be generous is to give one's time, talents, ultimately what one is.

Let us come back to Padre Penda to illustrate this point. Padre Penda has graduated from the University of the Mountain. He is now a Master of

---

[11] Harambee is a Kenyan tradition of community self-help. The word means "all pull together in Swahili. The term is on the Kenya coat-of-arms and is the nation's official motto.

Divinity degree. He starts reading for the doctoral degree. From May to July he concentrates on his study of ministry without doing any ministry. He is receiving without giving. After the summer school period, he suffers from intellectual and spiritual indigestion. He then discovers that the only solution to his sickness is to give of himself. He has no money to give. He then calls one of his most intimate friends, Stan Persons, the Vicar of St. Stephens Church in Bon Secour, Alabama. He asks for the work without pay. Stan arranges for him to preach to his two Churches and work in the youth camp. Padre Penda is the first Black priest to preach in these Churches. However, this is not the most important issue for him. The important thing is self-giving. He also needs to be healed as he heals others. The theme of his sermon is: "Jesus is the bread of life." In this introduction, he is very open to his hearers. He says, "I am suffering from spiritual indigestion. For three months, I have been receiving without giving. I have been accumulating knowledge without sharing it with others. Therefore, one of the reason why I am in this pulpit is to be healed by you." At these remarks, the Spirit of God comes mightily to Padre Penda and the congregation. The whole Church is filled with the dwelling-of-God-with-his-own. Penda is healed. His hearers, too, are healed. Indeed, Jesus the bread of life, is feeding the hungry hearts.

On Tuesday of that week, Stan is taking Padre Penda to the youth camp. They are driving to the camp site. Suddenly Penda is surrounded by young, black faces! He was not expecting Black campers. They too never dreamed of meeting an African. All the counselors except one are white. These poor boys come from the inner-city. Their behavior is very much like that of the parking boys whom he used to rehabilitate at Nakuru. Their level of trust is very low. The counselors and the camp Director have real concern and love for these boys and girls. However, for the first three days the youngsters are ambivalent about the white counselors and their African brother. In their eyes, Padre Penda looks like African snakes, bees, jungle, primitive man, and a tribal warrior. Most of them fear him greatly. One girl for instance, who could not stand near Padre Penda for three days, accidentally met him near the

THE HOLY SPIRIT

dining hall. She sees him and stands four yards away from him. In order to help her overcome fear, Padre Penda says,

"You look nice."

"Do you still eat people in Africa?" the girl asked suspiciously.

Before Padre Penda replies, the girl turns and runs away. Padre Penda is left alone thinking. He learns that he is symbolizing that part of the American Negroes which have made them suffer and be socially stigmatized for three hundred years.

Nevertheless, Penda and the other counselors have long-suffering-love. They give themselves to the youngsters. They fought their fear and doubt by being amiable, and by playing and swimming with them. Anger, which Penda's C.P.E. peers were advising him to adopt is the weakest weapon. It is rarely used. The counselors are struggling to love and identify themselves with the youngsters. On the fourth evening the counselors and the campers have something similar to the Kikuyu initiation dances known as 'Mararanja' (sleeping away from the house). They put on crowns. They wear masks and act crazy. The counselors participate in the precariousness and tension of the boys and girls. The attitude of these youngsters is changed. They are now trusting and loving and accepting of their African brother. The sixth night was Padre Penda's night. He is enthroned. All the teams play Padre Penda's role. Let us hear what Penda says about the experience,

> The most impressive things were the gifts which they gave me, all of which they had made with their hands. The most remarkable of these gifts was a piece of paper with the drawing of my heart with all their names in it and the following words: 'Padre Penda, big and strong-hearted man, who we all love for his courage and braveness. Love always.' That was the nicest gift I had ever received in my life. These beloved Negroes and poor white boys and girls gave of their

very best. They gave me their names, better still, their very beings. Indeed, they gave me God!"

This is what Paul means by gentleness. Padre Penda had no money to give. But he had himself and his gifts. These were more valuable than money to the campers and the Christians of St. Stephen Church. Stan, on the other hand had work to give to Padre Penda. The work gave Penda spiritual inspiration and a sense of worth. Stan was generous with work. He also took the risk of inviting a Black Padre to preach in his congregation. The white counselors also showed gentleness and generosity. They generously gave a whole evening to Padre Penda. They prepared the youngsters to play the role of Padre Penda. And they reconciled the Afro-American, with their Africanness.

What we are saying in this section is that, gentleness, kindness, generosity as the fruit of the Holy Spirit is more than giving material things. A Christian should not have self-pity just because he does not have thousands of shillings[12] to give publicly in Harambee. He is only required to give that which he has. Yet if one is blessed with material things, this fruit of the spirit will lead him to give to those in need.

To be gentle, kind and generous in the Sprit means: "that which I have, I freely give." One feels good by giving that which he has.

---

[12] Kenyan currency.

THE HOLY SPIRIT

6. **Goodness**

One of the nickname of Padre Penda was Son of Goodness(Wanyakiega). Nyakiega was the name of his great-grandmother. She got this name because she was so hospitable and generous that she gave her food to whoever visited her. And she would weep if the food was depleted and had nothing to give.

Goodness is another fruit of the Holy Spirit. This fruit of the Spirit means more than just doing good or ethical perfection. It is not merely turning the other check. It does not even imply that the Church which is indwelt by the Spirit will only preach and talk about the goodness of God. There was a very interesting discussion among a group of teenagers in a youth camp at Mount Eagle. This group which was led by Padre Penda was discussing the fruit of the Holy Spirit. The dialogue between Penda and Mary went as follows:

	Mary: I hate this fruit
Penda:	"Which fruit?"
Mary:	"Goodness"
Penda:	"Why?"
Mary:	Because it reduces God to goodness."
Penda:	"So you don't believe that God is goodness?"
Mary:	"I don't think so. Moreover, I am fed up with the preaching in the Church because the minister preaches nothing but goodness. If God is goodness, why is it that there is so much evil in the world?"
Penda:	"So you think if God is good he must do away with all evil in the world?"
Mary:	"If God is good, there must be goodness in the whole world. If evil exists in the world, it then follows that God does not exist."

Mary was raising a very important point. She was questioning the notion that, "God is goodness and goodness is God." Of course, the Bible indicates that God has both negative and positive characteristics. He loves and gets angry. He feels jealousy if we worship another god. Being God's creatures, we too, have both negative and positive aspects. We cannot always be positive. Moreover, to be in the Spirit does not imply that everything will be good and that we will move in life victoriously. Life is a mystery. It is full of ordeals and pain. Furthermore, we have seen that the Holy Spirit, like Mutiiri, does not avert pain, but helps us to confront pain with courage.

Nevertheless, this fruit of the Spirit enables us to live in accordance with Christian moral standards. It is connected with self-control. As the Book of Proverbs puts it:

> He who is slow to anger is better than the mighty.
>
> And he who rules his spirit than he who takes a city. Proverb 16:32

The Bible also connects goodness with beauty. Thus, a Christian who is always shaggy and shabby does not demonstrate this fruit of the Spirit. Since God is God of beauty, a Christian should be beautifully dressed particularly when going to church or to other gatherings. There is nothing wrong with a Christian woman going to a beauty shop and having her hair done. A Christian who bears the fruit of the Spirit should be as clean and as beautiful as possible. Remember that you cannot be too beautiful for God.

In addition, the gift which Paul speaks[13] about is the inner quality of life which springs from the Holy Spirit. It means to be and to do good. This quality of life is well expressed by a Kikuyu proverb: "A good word

---

[13] 1 Corinthians 12:1-11.

is better than gifts," meaning that gifts are nothing to the recipient if they are not accompanied by good words, or if they do not come from a good heart. This is in keeping with the teaching of Martin Luther who taught that good works should proceed from faith and like good fruits, prove that the man himself is already righteous at heart in God's sight. Goodness of the Spirit emerges from our hearts. It is a faithful goodness.

7. Faithfulness

It is this fruit of the Spirit which enables us to believe, to trust, to put faith in and to rely on God. It has an idea of the Mutiiri who is given complete trust and obedience. As we have seen, Mutiiri nurses, teaches and guides the initiate. The initiate in turn complies with the Mutiiri. The Spirit likewise, helps us to obey and trust in God. He also helps us to trust ourselves and our fellow men. Some people will never trust because they do not get trust from society. As one of my Negro friends said as he shared his pain: "Tell them the truth, but they will never believe you until they go to hell." Christians, who are the temple of the Holy Spirit are obliged to facilitate trust to those who have been maimed and crippled by society. We have to illuminate them by our faithfulness. We have to heal their wounds as they heal ours. A faithful man is also a humble man.

8. Humility

The gift of the Holy Spirit is clearly seen in the life of Padre Penda. During his work among the "parking boys" in Nakuru, he identified himself with them, and humbly accepted being labeled as a 'dustbin.'

To be humble in the Spirit means to soften, to appease, to make mild or gentle. It also means to soothe, calm, and tame. If two people are fighting, this fruit of the Spirit will enable us to calm them down. It will help us to reconcile and tame them.

However, humility does not mean self-pity. It is not being unassertive or losing oneself in the climate of public opinion. The Spirit does not even expect one to lose oneself in marriage. The Spirit helps us to treat others as we would like them to treat us. He enables us to soothe others by sharing our weakness with them. This does not make us weak and less influential. In my life, the individuals who have exerted a great influence and have changed my life are those who have shared their weakness with me. As with Padre Penda, humility implies identifying ourselves with those who are socially outcast. Our Master demonstrated this quality of life by eating with sinners and tax collectors. Mark 2:13-17, Matthew 9:10.

Humility of the Spirit will lead us to doing those duties which will never put us on the front page of the Newspaper. We perform duties like visiting the poor, the orphans, the widows, the elderly, and the lonely. Humility means service. This is why Jesus advised his disciples that he who wants to be great must be the servant of all. Mark 9:35. This fruit also helps us to admit that we are wrong when we are wrong. As a Swahili proverb advises, "Asiyekubali kushindwa si mshindani," that is, "He who does not admit defeat is not a fighter." Humility is not without a reward. Jesus says, "Blessed are the meek, for they shall inherit the earth." Matthew 5:5.

We cannot be humble without self-control.

9. Self-Control

Lastly, comes self-control. The meaning of the original Greek work includes temperance and discipline. Self-control as a fruit of the Holy Spirit is not simply sobriety or a low level of sex-drive, although the restraint of gluttony and lust will surely be aspects of its effect upon behavior. Self-control will be evident equally in the manner in which a person pursues individual goals or supports the aim of the group.

Self-control is in keeping with African philosophy of life. For instance, most African initiations train young men and women to exercise self-control. For example, a Kikuyu initiate was expected to control his or her feelings and emotion when he was being operated upon. Bodily movement was not allowed.

During the seclusion one was trained to live in the community. The fruit of self-control will determine the way in which we live with and treat others. This fruit of the Spirit will control the expression of anger so that it does not work destructively. It can help us to live according to our dream, "I am because we are; and since we are therefore I am." This fruit of the Spirit enables us to live in and as a community by forgiving and forbearing each other.

The fruits of the Spirit are not alien to African soil. They Spirit of God was at work long before the Missionaries came to Africa. Moreover, some African people addressed God as the 'Great Spirit.'

CHAPTER THIRTEEN

THE HOLY SPIRIT IN TRADITIONAL RELIGIONS

Some African societies describe God as "Active Spirit." "The Creative Spirit," and the "Saving Spirit." Other communities address God in their prayer as simply, the Great Spirit. This is well illustrated by a Shona[14] hymn which they sang to God when praying for the rain:

> Great Spirit
> Pile-up of the rock into towering mountains …!
> Who seweth the heaven like cloth…?
> Caller forth of the branching tree
> Thou bringest forth the shoots
> That they stand erect.
> Thou fillest the land with mankind,
> The dust raise on high O Lord,
> Wonderful One,
> Thou livest in the midst of the sheltering rocks,
> Thou givest of rain to mankind

---

[14] A group of peoples living in Southern African countries.

> We pray to thee.
> Hear us, Lord!
> Show mercy when we beseech thee, Lord.
> Thou art on high in the Spirit of the great.
> Thou raisest the grass, covered hills
> Above the earth and greatest rivers,
> Gracious One!

The above hymn depicts the Great Spirit as a person. The personal pronoun "thou" is repeated six times. This implies that the Shona believed the Great Spirit has relationship with mankind. Being a person, he can be delighted or angry with us. He talks to us and we can also talk to him. Acts 8:29, 16:7. The Spirit can feel in and with us. He intercedes for us.

Furthermore, our prayer exhibits the Great Spirit as God. Many African people conceive God as the Spirit and for this reason they have no image of God. We all ask with the Pygmy:

> "Who can make an image of God
> He has no body
> He is a word which comes out of your mouth."[15]

As a God, the Holy Spirit has all the substance of God. As article V in the Book of Common Prayer[16] has it:

"The Holy Ghost, proceeding from the Father and the Son, is of one substance, majesty and glory with the Father and the Son, very and eternal God."[17] So the Holy Spirit has the same quality with God the

---

[15] John S. Mbiti, *Concepts of God in Africa*, London S.P.C.K., 1970, pp. 23-24.

[16] *The Book of Common Prayer*, London: Collins Clear-Type Press) p. 562.

[17] *Ibid.*

Father and God the Son. As God, he can be worshipped and glorified. He is exalted because he is "on high in the Spirit of the Great." He also connects our soul with the Supreme Being who is both and at the same time, transcendent and immanent.

The Shona ascribe fertility and creative power to the Great Spirit. Similarly, the Old Testament makes it clear the Spirit participated in creation. He brought form out of the formless chaos. He creates man and the heavens and sustains animal life. Genesis 1:1-3, 2:7, Job 26:13, Psalm 104:30.

In the New Testament, the Spirit is the creative agent of the second Adam. Better still, He possesses the quality of Eros. Matthew tells us: "Now the birth of Jesus Christ took place in this way. When his mother Mary had been betrothed to Joseph, before they came together, she was found to be with child of the Holy Spirit." Matthew 1:18. Luke also demonstrates the erotic attribute of the Holy Spirit in the conversation of the angel Gabriel and Mary. The angel said to Mary: "And behold, you will conceive in your womb and bear a son, and you shall call his name Jesus." Matthew 1:13. Since Mary had no husband she asked the angel how these things would be. The angel Gabriel answered:

> The Holy Spirit will come upon you
> And the power of the Most High will overshadow you;
> Therefore the child to be born will be called
> holy, the Son of God

One of the greatest errors of East African Christianity, which is heavily influenced by the East African Revival Movement, is to equate spirituality with asexuality. When I was six years of age, I overheard my mother and her friend discussing the sexual relationship between my mother and father. The question which was posed to my mother, the preacher's wife, was, "How do you get children?" "Why?" my mother asked. "Is your husband not a preacher?", my mother's friend asked.

"No one is righteous in sex affairs," my mother responded. My mother's friends could not see any connection between the pulpit and sexuality. Similarly, many Christians in East Africa confuse the relationship between God's love and Eros. A Christian is expected to show God's love but not Eros. Any act which manifests human sexuality is condemned. Two persons of the opposite sex are not expected to walk together unless they are husband and wife. In some areas, a husband cannot sit together with his wife in the Church. There is the female side and the male side in the Church. Holiness is equated with asexuality.

If we hold that there is nothing God has not given, and nothing which is not given, we will not find it hard to accept that sexuality is God-given. This is so because God does not give that which he does not possess. I do believe that it is the erotic quality of the Holy Spirit which draws us to God. This quality gives us a desire for God and a warm feeling toward other people, regardless of their sex. It fills us with warmth, intimacy, tenderness, and cordiality.

CHAPTER FOURTEEN

CONCLUSION

This book has shown that the Holy Spirit resides and operates in and through human persons. The Holy Spirit works in the Ministers of the Gospel (both lay and ordained) who minister in the power of the Holy Spirit. As a Mutiiri, the Holy Spirit is a dynamic presence, counselor, teacher, comforter, advocate, and reconciler. While He is always with us, the presence of the Holy Spirit is felt in a special way during our life crises and our spiritual developmental stages and when we are undertaking challenging mission.

We have also seen that there is no spiritual gift which is compulsory to all Christians. Since the body does not consist of one member, we should not exalt one of the gifts of the Holy Spirit at the cost of the other gifts. We should also not dismiss a particular gift because it has been overemphasized by a particular denomination.

The author made a very interesting observation. He is a great friend of Padre Penda. Padre and his wife occasionally worship at Pentecostal Holiness Church. This denomination separated from Church of Nazarene. The two groups disagreed on the speaking in tongue in the church. The former allowed speaking in tongue during the worship while the latter eschewed the speaking in tongue in the church. What surprised Penda was that all the times he attended Pentecostal Holiness Church, he never saw anybody speaking in tongue. He was, however, surprised by a Sudanese Nazreen church pastored by his Seminary Student. There was prophetic utterance and praying in tongue. Penda and his wife, overwhelmed by the Holy Spirit, prayed in prayer language. Penda's prayer language comes with tears while his wife speaks in tongues without tears. He was also surprised to see other worshippers whose prayer language is tear. There was freedom of the Holy Spirit and as Paul put it, where there is Holy Spirit there is freedom. 2 Corinthians 3:17, Prayer language is manifestation of the Holy Spirit. And he manifests himself in many ways. As St. Paul puts it: "Now to each one the manifestation of the Spirit is given for the common good." 1 Corinthians 12:7. God gives us many gifts for the edification of the body of Christ: The Bible puts it this way: " "To one there is given through the Spirit the message of wisdom, to another the message of knowledge by means of the same Spirit, to another faith by the same Spirit, to another the gifts of healing by that one Spirit, to another miraculous power, to another prophecy, to another distinguishing between the spirits, to another speaking is the different kinds of tongues, and to still another the interpretation of tongues. All these are works of one and the same Spirit, and he gave them to each one just as he determines" 1 Corinthian 12:8-11. As we have discussed, I have been surprised by the diversity of gifts of the Spirit.

I remember one time having a cough that was coming out with blood. I had just come from a very challenging mission to Sri Lanka. Coming home, I had congestion and then the coughing up of blood. I tried to treat myself, without success. Finally, I talked to myself, "John, you are a D.min not an MD," so I visited my doctor who did a thorough examination, including a blood test, and then recommended that I see a chest specialist. Before I left the office, I asked: "Doc, where is my prescription?" He said: "You can do better all by yourself." Coming home,

THE HOLY SPIRIT

I called Bishop Steven, our Bishop in the United Kingdom, and reported the disease. Bishop Evan prayed for me and I was instantaneously healed. When I went to the chest specialist, he confirmed that I was completely healed and that I did not need any medicine.

Another surprise of the Holy Spirit happened unexpectedly. It was early in the morning when I was taking garbage out to the dumpster. As I opened the door I saw two white faces-a man and a woman. I took the garbage back to let them in. It turns out that they were Jews who have travelled 500 miles to visit with us. So, after they have introduced themselves, Mary gave them breakfast. We shared many things which included our ministries and the Spiritual gifts. The husband was a prophet and the wife was a seer. Even though I have five theological degrees, I have not yet distinguished between a prophet and a seer. So, I had to learn about this from our guests. After visiting for four hours, our guest prayed for us. The seer saw that Mary was having problems with her lower back. She volunteered to pray for Mary. To Mary's greatest surprise, the seer touched the spot which had bothered her for a long time. When she was praying, Mary felt warmth on that spot. She was completely healed. Taking the couple to the class, I asked them to pray and prophesy to the students. Among other things, the Seer prophesy to a Nubian student that his ministry is to reach out to the Muslims. And this was also the vision of this student. He invites the Muslims family for Christmas and the Muslims outnumber Christian. This information was revealed to a Seer by the Holy Spirit.

A call out of a denomination with which I ministered for many years was predicted to a prophetess who didn't know me. She was a prayer partner of my sister in law, Margret. While they were praying, Martha asked Margret: "who is this John I am seeing." "John is my brother in law" Margret restored. "His ministry with the church he is ministering is coming to end." When Margret called, and told me about the prophecy, I was apprehensive because at that time everything was going on well. Two years later, the prophecy was fulfilled. The call to establishing All

Nations Christian Church International was prophesied by my student, Skip. He saw me flying high as an eagle. My eye sight was very sharp and I was seeing the snake on the ground, which I was killing. My wife remained on the ground and was keeping me steady on the ground. I was followed by likeminded eagles as we were flying to what appeared like endless destination." The prophecy was fulfilled and it is still being fulfilled. Both Martha and Skip were ordained by our hands and are our affiliates.

I was surprised by the Holy Spirit when Bishop Tom Brown and I was ministering in the Living Faith Church which is ministered by our Bishop, Steven Evans. I was sitting on the front seat with Tom who was to deliver the Word. Bishop Tom knelt to pray so as to prepare his heart for the empowerment of the Holy Spirit. A lady who came and knelt with him, rested in Spirit and I had to hold her so that she could fall gently without hurting herself. Patriarch became the armor bearer of his bishop.

We have also been astonished by the Holy Spirit during our overseas ministry. We had a mission trip to Kenya with a team of seven missioners, which included my wife, our son Isaac, Dr. Leon and Mrs. Whitaker. We ministered in three dioceses, four public schools, and Karura parish, in which I ministered before coming to United States. One of the miracles was gathering together more than a thousand students without a prior notice. The Spirit showed sign and wonders. In Kitale, Mary healed a woman who was possessed by demon. Isaac, who was nine years old, preached at the open-air service. The greatest surprise took place at St. Philips in Kihara. This church was nicknamed "Elephant Stomach" because of its size and the membership. Ironically, this church's congregation boycotted the last Holy Communion that I had to give them before coming to USA. They complained that the vice chairman had not informed them ahead of time so as to prepare their heart. I am now coming back a decade later.

After the sermon, I asked those who have not yet received Christ as the personal Savior and those who want to receive a double portion of the Holy Spirit to come forward. I then knelt down and closed my eyes to pray. The Holy Spirit fell mightily and I stared weeping. When I opened the eyes, I saw two hundred people knelling on the hard floor. They were all filled with the Holy Spirit. One person who was closest to me rested in Spirit and laid on the floor for some time. Knocking people down has never been my expectation. But the Holy Spirit performs signs and wonders in whichever way He will. We are like a pen in his hand and he writes whenever He wants and whatever He wants.

Another big amazement occurred when the mission team returned to USA. Dr Leon Whitaker, a retired Vice President at Grambling State University, organized a prayer breakfast at one of the University buildings. It was attended by three hundred university employees. There was a heavy anointment of the Holy Spirit. Once again, I wept uncontrollably. I saw the glory of God in the public institution that is not norm in American public Institutions. I also wept for perceiving that the missioners came back being more transformed than the people they ministered. I was also moved to tear because of the prophet's reward. By taking people who were not members of my denomination, I was accused by the Lay Pope that I had become two ecumenical. Consequently, I lost a third of my compensation.

I was also transformed and moved far beyond my community norm. According to Kikuyu and many other African peoples, a circumcised person does not cry in public. When I was teaching at St Paul's University, we had a heated discussion in pastoral class about weeping during a funeral. A Rwandese student argued that it is the work of the priest to see to it that people don't cry during the funeral. I then referred to him the shortest verse in the Bible: "Jesus Wept." John 11:35. The student responded. "That was the only time that Jesus committed sin." As Christians, we are not expected to be more Christian than Christ. Of course, therapeutically, the best way to deal with a weeping person is to hold her shoulders and let her weep and weep and weep. Better still, weep with her for the Bible advises us to "Weep with those who weep." Romans 12:15. However, our major subject is about the manifestation of Holy Spirit. His activity is manifested in us in whichever way He wills.

Another interesting episode in which I was stunned by the Holy Spirit took place at St. John's Church in Karura. I was visiting with bishop after the service when we were interrupted by a parishioner. "Please, I want to tell you about my ministry;" he urged. "Go ahead." I responded. "My ministry is to buy Christian books and give them to a group or a person who needs the book." "You have come to the right person. I am looking for a book entitled Bishop Facing Mount Kenya;" I said. The parishioner opened his brief case and that was the only book he had. And so he gave it to me.

In this year, 2016, we were astonished by the way the Holy Spirit used Pastor Peter Palani, our affiliate from India. Peter, Like Paul, supports himself by being a taxi driver and then ministers the marginalized community. Peter's six days with us in Texas were characterized by mutual impartation. We were surprised by so many gifts that he brought to us; most of which had gospel messages. He gave us key holders with messages such as: "Keep me as the apple of your eye; From this day I will bless you; I am the Good Shepherd; God bless you; and For I am the Lord who heals." The most surprising gift was a pregnant elephant that reminded me of the dream I had when I was planning for the mission to India. In the dream, I saw myself carrying a live elephant on my back. In addition to the gifts, Peter surprised us when we were taking him sightseeing at Palo Duro Park. He volunteered to pay for the entrance fees. The Lord enjoyed fulfilling his promise "Give and it shall be given unto you." Luke 6:38. Our Seminary[18] students, most of

---

[18] All Nations Christian Church International (ANCCI) University Seminary, Canyon, Texas.

THE HOLY SPIRIT

who are refugees with limited income, gave Peter $300 for three bikes for his pastors.

After preaching and administering healing in a Congolese Congregation pastored by our Seminary Student Eliazard, all of who are refugees with minimal income, its members donated 11 bikes for the Indian Pastors. Other members donated money for the orphanage. One Congolese said; "Since you are my size and I have another suit and a pair of shoes, that will be my gifts to you." A lady said: "Since we love you so much and we want you to look smart, and I sell suits, I will buy one suit for you." St. Cyprian's International Church in Amarillo prepared the consecration service and reception for Peter. We indeed experienced anointing of the Holy Spirit. Besides consecration, Patriarch, using the principles of an analytical psychologist, helped Peter identify his personality type, which is ISFJ: "if you are ISFJ, you belong to 6 per cent of the population. Even though you appear quiet, reserved, down -to- earth; you are sensible, orderly, neat, gentle, humane, super-dependable and you can be good….at ministering to the needy, marginalized and ignorant people" (See Initiation and Pastoral Psychology, Toward African Personality Theory, p,155.) Interesting, Bishop Peter ministers to the leper,[19] blind, orphaned and windowed. This indeed was the ministry of the Messiah who was full of the Holy Spirit. When the John the Baptist sent his disciples to check out whether Jesus was the messiah, Jesus responded:

---

[19] Leprosy, also known as Hansen's disease is a long-term bacterial infection. The infection is initially asymptomatic and usually remains so for five to 20 years. "Leprosy Fact Sheet". *World Health Organization. Jan 2014.* Leprosy is spread between people, perhaps through a cough or contact with fluid from the nose of an infected person. However, despite popular belief, it is not highly contagious and is curable with multidrug therapy. Leprosy occurs more commonly among those living in poverty. In India, the risk of social rejection is so great that many people cured of leprosy end up living in isolated settlements. As of 2007, there were more than 1,000 leprosy colonies in India. BBC News, on-line at http://news.bbc.co.uk/2/hi/programmes /from_our_ own_correspondent/6510503.stm.

"Go back and report to John what you have seen and heard: the blind receive sight, the lame walk, those who have leprosy are cleansed, the deaf hear, the dead are raised and the good news is being proclaimed to the poor." Luke 7:22.

This suffices to show that all the gifts are the impartation of the Holy Spirit for the common good. They are for building up and maintaining the body of Christ. As Paul writes:

> Now you are the body of Christ,
> and individually members of it.
> And God has appointed in his Church
> first apostles, second prophets,
> third teachers, the workers of miracles,
> then the healers, helpers, administrators,
> speakers in various kinds of tongues
> Are all apostles?
> Are all prophets?
> Are all teachers?
> Do all work miracles?
> Do all possess gift of healing?
> Do all speak with tongues?
> Do all interpret? 1 Corinthians 12:27-30.

The answer to these rhetorical questions is no. All of us cannot be priests or teachers. We should not expect every Christian to speak with tongues.

Nevertheless, we have argued that every Christian is expected to bear all the fruits of the Holy Spirit. All those who are born of the Spirit should be loving, joyful, peaceful, patient, kind, good, faithful, and self-controlled.

We have also noted that the Spirit has persuasive and attractive qualities, which draw and help us to cleave to God. He is also a person who relates to us in a personal way. Furthermore, He is God who has all the qualities of God the Father, and God the Son; yet, He is distinguished from them. When He comes in us, the Spirit comes with the totality of a God who "in many ways and various ways spoke of old to our fathers by the prophets, but in these last days he has spoken to us by a Son, whom he appointed the heir of all things, through whom also he created the world." Hebrews 1:1-3.

www.ingramcontent.com/pod-product-compliance
Lightning Source LLC
LaVergne TN
LVHW050134080526
838202LV00061B/6486